Bea Longing

Emily learns change is hard

part one

EMILY BEA LONG

Illustrated By

MICHELLE MCDONALD

AuthorHouse™
1663 Liberty Drive
Bloomington, IN 47403
www.authorhouse.com
Phone: 833-262-8899

This book is printed on acid-free paper.

ISBN: 978-1-6655-2183-3 (sc)
978-1-6655-2184-0 (e)

Print information available on the last page.

Published by AuthorHouse 04/13/2021

authorHOUSE®

Dedicated to...

Grannie,
You Said It's Okay To Be Different.

Ariana Di Diana,
You Believed In Me.

Grace Tranc,
You Said Not To Worry.

Uncle John,
You Read Me A Story.

My Parents, Debbie and George,
You Gave Me Your Everything.

And Elmwood Park,
The Community I Belong To.

TABLE OF CONTENTS

CHAPTER ONE
LIFE IS GOOD...SO SHE THOUGHT.

HI! I'm Emily Bea Long.
Please allow me to introduce myself.
I have good grades and I work hard to make my parents proud.

I like to play with garden gnomes and I laugh really loud.
I'm student council president and a bit goofy.
I'm always pleasant, and when my teacher calls on me I say 'present'!

I live in a place outside Chicago.
Have you heard of Elmwood Park?
It's just like any other place.

We have firefighters, police officers, doctors and nurses,
construction workers, bankers,
grocery clerks, lawyers, and teachers.
My town is filled with all sorts of great people!

I like to crack jokes, eat moon pies,
and ride my blue tricycle around town.
My dream is to be
Elmwood Park's Best Singer!

But then my life changed.

"Hey, I'm Ariana!
I'll take the story from here.
I'm Emily's best friend,
I want to make that clear."

"Ariana back off!
This is my story to tell."

"Yeah, but Emily,
you don't tell it well!"

"Oy! You're pressing my buttons."

"Whatever, Emily, now let me begin!"

The year is 2020 and in March her world turned upside down.
Suddenly Emily had reason to frown.

People were sent
home from work,

she couldn't see grandma
until further notice,

and her mom's nights at
the hospital grew longer.

People purchased toilet
paper in big packages.

It seemed like Halloween wasn't just one time a year.

School was over too...so she thought.
Her dreams were over, gone down the drain.

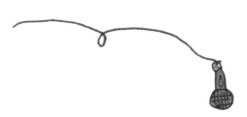

She was forced to sit and wonder:
Will E-Swizzely come out from under?

No summer vacation,
Mom bought a pool for home this year.
Emily tried to make summer not drag,
she was about ready to throw in the rag.

Mom and dad turned on the news.
Emily thought to herself:

"What The Heck Is Covid-19...
And Why Is It Giving Everyone The Blues?!?!?"

Her mom said not to worry,
wash your hands, and use sanitizer in a hurry.

Emily did as she was told, but the nights grew cold.
She had no friends.
She lost her strive to be bold.
And staying home was getting OLD.

She needed change, her world was dark.

Emily wished for a little spark.

School started,
it was different this time,
she could only see her friends and teacher online!

Emily disliked being home.
She missed her clubs.

She imagined the school's bathroom
stalls stunk like nobody's poo.

And Mrs. Worbly's gross cafeteria
food seemed good too.

Emily Bea Long started to feel like she didn't belong.

CHAPTER TWO

ALL BETS ARE OFF
WHEN A PANDEMIC STRIKES.

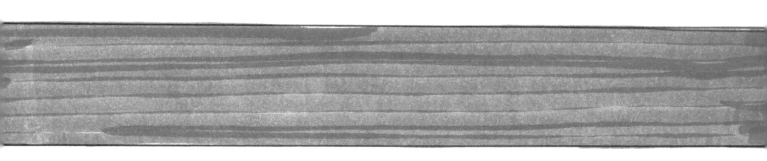

ONE day Emily creeped up the stairs, she overheard some talking.
Mom and dad were at it again.
"The office needs me."
"I can't do everything."

2020 bore on her family.
There was so much change.
It was too much to ignore.

Emily felt sad.
It was all her fault.
E-learning was too hard.
What would be the result?

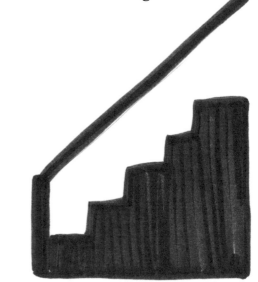

She didn't care about the world or school anymore.
She grabbed her things and walked out the door.

Emily would be Elmwood Park's Best Singer, despite what other people would think.
She didn't need e-learning.

Her tricycle went CLIIIIINNNNK!!!!!

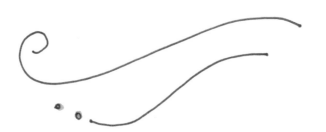

"I'm going to make something of myself.
No one needs school.
I'll make people happy again, just you watch,
I'm nobody's fool."

Emily was determined to make her dreams come true.
There had to be something she could do.
People needed to come together.
She wanted life to be a tiny bit better.

CHAPTER THREE
GRAB LIFE BY THE COCONUTS.

RIDING a tricycle made her bones feel brittle.
Emily felt like a grannie, so she sat to ponder a little.
A delivery driver approached.
He wasn't sure what to make of a girl alone at the park.
After all, it WAS the afternoon on a school day.
He was dropping off groceries curbside.

THE man looked from his right to his left.
"Hey kid, why are you wallowing," he said.
"Where's your mom?"
He tried to guess.
"Shouldn't you be in school?"

He giggled at how she dressed.
It was different, unique.

"I hate e-learning and I'm running away from home.
No one can stop me! Leave me alone!"

The driver got down on his knee and tried to explain.
"I'm sorry friend, I hear you out.
I understand why you pout.
I had another job, but then a pandemic hit.

My boss sent me home forever and said I couldn't come back.
I wore a suit and tie to work.
Now, I carry packages all day long.
Sometimes you have to try new things and fight change head on."

Emily kind of understood what he was trying to say,
but she couldn't give in just yet.
She wanted things her way.

"You can't get me to learn if I don't want to.
I have a dream and I don't need school.
No one believes in me, but I do.
I'm going to be Elmwood Park's Best Singer."

The delivery driver attempted to call the police.
Emily knew if she stayed her dream would cease.
So, as he turned his back,
She was gone in a flash.

"I'm never going home!"
She didn't look back.

CHAPTER FOUR

WOULD I LOOK GOOD
IN A RED HAT TOO?

EMILY likes to hang in the circle,
one time she swears she saw a fox!
She put her tricycle away,
and sat on a bench next to the bus.

A lady in yellow wearing a red hat appeared.
Emily said to herself, "Don't say anything, this lady looks weird."
"Where are you going, Little Miss?" said the old lady.
Emily didn't want to talk, but what else did she have to do?

The lady's snottiness didn't seem right,
But her eyes glistened with delight.
She figured why not,
It's not like she'd bite.

"I'm going to follow my dream," said Emily.
The old lady chuckled, took out her hand, and waved it around.
"Well I'm going to be an astronaut, how does that sound?"
She waited a moment.
Then said, "Call me Miss Kathy."

"Was this woman a sorcerer?
Is she a witch who will grant me my wish?" thought Emily.
She was inches away and leaned a few inches toward her.
Miss Kathy was nice, so a quick justification would suffice.

"I'm not like everyone else.
I'm different, I swear!
I'm special and I have talent!" said Emily.

"Of course you are!
"Everyone in E-P is special.
Everyone in Chicago is special.
Everyone in the world is special!"

Emily's heart felt warm and fuzzy inside.
"Yeah they are...
and so am I...
and so are YOU!" she replied.

Kathy scoffed, a bit jaded by life,
"I guess you're right kid!
Too many people these days are
trying to tell you nobody matters."
Miss Kathy glanced at her watch.
"Shouldn't you be in school?"

"Yeah, but I'm tired of learning.
Everything is on a link and they expect me
to do it all on my own," said Emily.

There was something different in the way she was now speaking.
A crack quivered deep down, she wasn't as angry as it seemed.

"It's...it's...it's overwhelming."

"I see, I see. Have you thought about going outside or maybe creating an incentive for yourself?" said Miss Kathy.

"What's an incentive?"

"When you have a goal, you take baby steps to get there.
You give yourself a pat on the back for every step you accomplish.
Besides, to be a singer don't you need music sales?"

Emily looked up.

"Yeah," she said.

"How do you plan to do that if you don't know your times tables or arithmetic?" said the older lady.

"Arithmetic?!" exclaimed Emily.

She hadn't heard that word before.

"It's a synonym for math," said Miss Kathy.

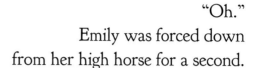

"Oh."
Emily was forced down
from her high horse for a second.

"What I'm saying is this," said Kathy.
"I have two chocolate bars.
One for me, and one for you.
What would we do if either of us wanted both?"

"I don't know."
Emily realized Miss Kathy was smarter than her.

"We could cut it in halves, or fourths, or eighths.
These are called fractions."

Betrayal rose up inside, Emily could see what she had done.
Miss Kathy had taught her something, she had given up one-plus-one!
This lady tricked her, so she exhausted the fiery breath of a dragon at the top of her lungs.

"YOU TRICKED ME, AND THAT'S NOT FAIR!!"

The bus arrived, just in the nick of time. The lady wearing yellow and a red hat was ready to leave, unbothered by Emily's explosive wind chime.

"The world isn't fair, kid. Life is a game and everyone plays for a different team. Only lately, people have forgotten what matters most...and that is... their love for the sport."

Miss Kathy stepped onto the bus and stuck her head out the door.

"Go back home and try a bit harder before you realize it's too late."

The bus was gone. Emily didn't know what was next, she felt an icky feeling in her chest. Had she made a terrible mistake?

She shook her head and threw out those thoughts.
Emily had a dream to pursue, and a Johnnie's beef sandwich seemed awfully good too.

CHAPTER FIVE

GOODBYE SANDWICH, HELLO BRIGHT LIGHTS.

EMILY ate her snack in peace, with its juice running from her hands to her feet. A voice called out from around the corner, Emily leaped with glee. She hadn't seen her friend since quarantine made everything flee.

"Nikki!" she called out.

"Emily," her friend shouted.

Emily ran faster than a car. She needed to say hi and remember what it was like to not be afar. Then Nikki's car passed like a shooting star.

Step by step her shoes glided across the street. Her sandwich suddenly fell, what a treacherous feat. Again, another reason why the world was unfair. She left and rode along, her heart too somber to bear.
She thought she had left for all the right reasons, but being on her own kicked more than mom's spicy seasons.

SDJNDJFBVLDS!!
THUD-THUD-WHACK-SLAM-TING-WHIP-ZAP!!
The sounds of plowing rang in her ear.
A construction worker was near.
A familiar face, who could it be?
Was it her neighbor, Mr. Miranda?

BEEF SANDWICH!

"Hey, don't I know you?"

"Yeah. You're the kid who lives down the street" he said.

Emily was happy to see someone she knew, it happened when she was starting to feel blue. Maybe he would tell her she was right to go on her journey. He seemed like the type who knows not to worry.

"I'm going to be Elmwood Park's Best Singer," she said with integrity.
"What a wonderful dream to have," he said.
"Did you always know you wanted to be a construction worker?" she asked.
She liked his warm smile and friendly face. It felt good to talk to someone who finally understood, someone who came from a familiar place.
"I always knew I wanted to help people," Mr. Miranda replied. Emily thought his words were sweeter than pie!
"I want to make an impact like you everyday. I want to bring people together with a song. I want everyone to be happy again. Where do I start? I need them to know they belong."

The construction worker knew what to say. "You can start by being a good friend." Emily was shocked, it couldn't be that easy. She thought, "I don't need to carry a sign or something?"

"You don't have to be the biggest, the brightest, or even the best at anything to lend a helping hand. Showing others kindness and accepting them for who they are is the best thing you can do. Imagine if the world was just a little nicer."

"Maybe if my mom was a bit nicer I wouldn't have so many chores around the house. What a difference that would make!" said Emily.

They laughed together.

"I gotta get going, Mr. Miranda," said Emily.

"You betcha, kid.
I'm looking forward to seeing your name in bright lights one day.
You should never give up on your dream and remember this—all it takes is accepting others for who they are to make a difference."

CHAPTER SIX
ARIANA IS WOKE.

"**HERE'S** the good part." said Emily.

"Finally!" said Ariana,"I've been waiting for this!"

"This is the part where we meet."

"Yeah, so let me tell it. Okay?!"

"Jeez"said Emily.

"Soooo, here's the part where Emily leaves the construction worker and makes her way to my house.

Emily is riding her tricycle, no surprise there. LOL.

She makes her way to my house and this is the part where I knock some serious sense into her.

Let's fast forward to the good stuff."

"Guess what," said Emily as she jumped onto the couch.

Ariana turned and gasped without hesitation, " O-M-G. You had your first kiss!"

The tables turned and Ariana had no clue what Emily was about to do.

"No," she rolled her eyes with an attitude and smirk, "Boys have cooties and I don't like twerps. I can't wait for Christmas!"

Ariana looked in Emily's direction, baffled at what she had said.

"Why would Santa bring you gifts? You're acting like a dummy."

Emily couldn't believe what she was hearing. That's when Ariana spoke the harsh truth.

"You expect Santa to bring you gifts when you're not even trying your best in school, but you're the one who said you're nobody's fool."

Emily couldn't believe it.

First her mom, then the delivery driver, and now her best friend.

"O-MY-LANTA so what! I'm going to be the best singer in Elmwood Park. I don't need school."

"EMILYYY..."

"DUDEEEEE!!!!"

"SERIOUSLY?!?"

"YEAH, SERIOUSLY."

The pair were silent until Ariana decided to talk.

"I had fun in my class today. We wrote my friend Sam a note online for her birthday. It was super cool."

That's when Emily started to think maybe e-learning wasn't impossible.

"I guess that is pretty cool."

"Just because something is hard it doesn't mean you should give up or throw in the towel. Why can't you be Elmwood Park's Best Singer and e-learner? Why not try? If you tried a little bit harder maybe you'd see it's not that bad, it's just different....remember when I made you try hawaiian pizza?"

"Yeah, it was SO GOOD," Emily looked back at the thought.

"See. Sometimes leaving your comfort zone, even though it's hard, isn't always a bad thing. The same goes with wearing a mask."

"When did you become so woke? What do I do now?" said Emily.

"How about you go home to your mom?" said Ariana.

"You're right, I'll talk to you later."

Emily zoomed out and headed towards home. She wasn't ready to give up just yet.

About the Author

Emily Long is the author of the new children's book series Bea Longing. Emily is a daycare teacher where she found the inspiration for her first novel. She spends her days caring for students and reminding them their voice matters. Emily has a Bachelor of Science degree in Mass Media from Illinois State University. She knows her name is no coincidence-Emily Bea Long believes everyone belongs.

Visit www.emilybelonging.com to learn more.

Printed in the United States
by Baker & Taylor Publisher Services